Annie Imagines

Written by: Mary Elizabeth Smith
Illustrated by: Linda Carol Carter

Senigami Publishing
Beaverton, OR

Senigami Publishing
7875 SW Hillcrest Place
Beaverton, OR 97008
Inquires: senigamipublishing@gmail.com

1st printing

Illustrations: Linda Carol Carter
Cover and interior design by Anita Jones, Another Jones Graphics

ISBN: 978-1-7324405-4-8 hard cover book
ISBN: 978-1-7324405-5-5 soft cover book
ISBN: 978-1-7324405-3-1 ebook

Library of Congress Control #2018910564

Publisher's Cataloging-In-Publication Data
(Prepared by The Donohue Group, Inc.)

Names: Smith, Mary Elizabeth, 1948- author. | Carter, Linda Carol, 1953- illustrator.
Title: Annie imagines / author: Mary Elizabeth Smith ; illustrator: Linda Carol Carter.
Description: Beaverton, OR : Senigami Publishing, [2019] | Interest age level: 004-008. | Summary: When Annie thinks she sees fairies but isn't sure, she turns to Grandma for an explanation and reassurance. By inventing imaginative encounters, Grandma helps Annie to see things in a new way, allowing her creativity to soar.
Identifiers: ISBN 9781732440548 (hardcover) | ISBN 9781732440555 (softcover) | ISBN 9781732440531 (ebook)
Subjects: LCSH: Grandparent and child--Juvenile fiction. | Imagination--Juvenile fiction. | Creative ability in children--Juvenile fiction. | Self-confidence in children--Juvenile fiction. | CYAC: Grandparent and child--Fiction. | Imagination--Fiction. | Creative ability--Fiction. | Self-confidence--Fiction.
Classification: LCC PZ7.1.S642 An 2019 (print) | LCC PZ7.1.S642 (ebook) | DDC [E]--dc23

Printed in the United States of America

To my Mother, Anne, for providing a safe setting where I could explore varied experiences and make my own choices without judgement.

There once was a girl named Annie who was very curious. She thought she could see fairies and other magical things. Annie could almost hear their little wings flit around her room and see them shimmer in the light from her window.

But she wasn't sure.

Annie asked her Mother, "Mama do you believe in fairies?"

Mama said, "Hmm…that is a very good question, Annie. Why don't you ask Grandma?"

So she asked her Grandma.

Grandma listened quietly and smiled. "Come with me into the garden, Annie. I want to give you some special things."

"   This is fairy dust," said Grandma.

"The Hummingbird gets it
for me from the nighttime fairies.
It has special powers."

"Rose-colored glasses will help you see magical things."

"Kindness, magic and fairies are every-where, Annie," said Grandma.

"You just have to know where to look."

And then Grandma took Annie to the top of the hill behind her house to look at the clouds.

Grandma asked, "What do you see?"

14 Annie looked hard, then exclaimed, "An elephant. A rabbit.

A penguin! A horse…a castle…and the man in the moon!"   15

"And now you know, Annie, that ordinary items can change into other things.

What would you make with these things?"

"I made a hat with a newspaper."

" Your big towel makes the best magic cape."

"I made a crown with the soup can."

"The Pizza box becomes my warrior shield."

19

Grandma asked, "You know my old car—
the bus in my front yard—the one painted
with rainbows and sunbeams and waves?
It can be your playhouse."

Annie clapped her hands and said, "I'll
make it my special place!"

"I'll drive over with the fairies to visit you,"
Annie said. "Later, we can pick up Mama
and go to the beach."

Grandma agreed, "That's a great idea!"

Grandma said, "Annie, you are special and kind. And have a wonderful imagination— it can take you anywhere you want to go."

You see what everyone else sees... but you can think and imagine something different.

Individual and Group Activities for Home and Classroom

We can use our imagination in what we create, draw, see or share with others. What can you imagine?

❊ Like Annie and her grandmother on pages 14 and 15...when you are outside with your family, or at recess or just laying on the grass, look up at the clouds. What do you see? What do others see who are with you? Can you create a story about what is happening?

❊ Annie and her grandmother had a special van in their yard for adventures. Have you ever created a car, train, or plane out of chairs from your house or the classroom? Where will you go? What would you take with you? Who would go with you? Draw or tell about your adventure.

❊ Set up a tent or make a fort inside the house or in the backyard. What could you use to make it? Draw or tell about what might happen.

❊ Imagine you are having a party. What could you use from the list on the next page to make it special? Who can help you?

❊ When you are going to sleep at night, imagine going on an adventure. Where might you go? Who is there when you arrive? What do you take with you? Tell a story or use things from the list on the next page to show what happens.

❊ There are many things around the house or in the classroom that can become new things when you use your imagination. What could you create with things listed on the next page? You can use one thing or many things to create whatever you think and see. All your ideas are good and special.

We want to see what you made. Please take a picture and send it.
We will put many on our web site. On the picture please, put your first name, town or school.
Send to: senigamipublishing@gmail.com

26

Acorn caps
Beads & buttons
Beans
Bottle caps
Corn husks
Doilies
Duct tape
Egg cartons
Felt squares
Glue & crayons/paint
Marbles
Metal or wooden spoons
Noodles
Paper bags
Paper clips
Paper cups & plates
Paper towel rolls
Pipe cleaners
Playing cards
Popsicle sticks
Rocks
Seashells
String
Styrofoam balls
Tissue paper
Toothpicks

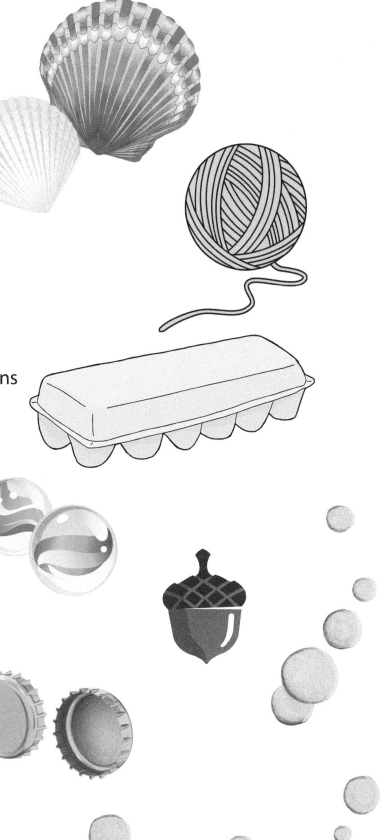

Mary Elizabeth Smith
Author and Publisher

With the rapid decline in our planet's environment, today's children need to develop the ability to perceive the world in new ways…find hidden patterns and make connections between unrelated phenomena that in turn can generate new ideas. Mary believes this is done through building children's confidence. Allowing them to freely express themselves and in turn, acknowledging their expression without judgment. In addition, it is important to surround children in an environment that is flexible and tolerant of vague, unclear expression that also embraces the unpredictable and fosters curiosity of the unknown.

Mary Elizabeth is a grandmother to nine grandchildren. She believes grandparents can be the mirror for children's fantastical imagination while gently guiding them into acceptance of their creative value. This kind of relationship can be a child's foundation for positive self-esteem, confidence and building aspirations for turning imagination into reality.

Mary Elizabeth resides in Beaverton Oregon. She can be reached through senigamipublishing@gmail.com

Linda Carol Carter
Illustrator

Linda Carol Carter has a wide, if not eclectic, range of creative, artistic talent and ability. She was born and raised in Southern California and graduated from Chapman University with a Bachelor's Degree in Art focusing on photography, drawing and painting.

Although art has been in Linda's genes from a very young age, she found her focus years later in Oregon, where she attended Portland's Oregon School of Arts and Crafts for advanced photography and studied advanced portrait work and Photoshop/Graphic Design at Pacific Northwest College of Art. She was also a participant in Gorge Artist Open Studios where she featured her large format acrylic paintings.

Linda's passion to work and paint from her own original photography is evident in her latest endeavor, *Annie Imagines*. Her illustrative nature and style, with an eye for minute detail, feeds, invites and encourages the imagination! Linda considers this collaboration with the author, a dear, old Northwest friend, a true joy.

Linda currently resides in Southern California, coming full circle.